The Peppermint Princess

Candy Fairies

Super Special

The Peppermint Princess

HELEN PERELMAN

ILLUSTRATED BY
ERICA-JANE WATERS

ALADDIN
NEW YORK LONDON TORONTO SYDNEY NEW DELHI

ALADDIN

An imprint of Simon & Schuster Children's Publishing Division

1230 Avenue of the Americas, New York, New York 10020

First Aladdin paperback edition October 2016

Text copyright © 2016 by Helen Perelman

Illustrations copyright © 2016 by Erica-Jane Waters

Also available in an Aladdin hardcover edition.

All rights reserved, including the right of reproduction in whole or in part in any form.

ALADDIN is a trademark of Simon & Schuster, Inc., and related logo is a registered
trademark of Simon & Schuster, Inc.

For information about special discounts for bulk purchases, please contact
Simon & Schuster Special Sales at 1-866-506-1949 or business@simonandschuster.com.

The Simon & Schuster Speakers Bureau can bring authors to your live event.
For more information or to book an event contact the Simon & Schuster
Speakers Bureau at 1-866-248-3049 or visit our website at www.simonspeakers.com.

Series designed by Karin Paprocki

Cover designed by Karina Granda

The text of this book was set in Berthold Baskerville Book.

Manufactured in the United States of America 0916 OFF

2 4 6 8 10 9 7 5 3 1

Library of Congress Control Number 2016936448

ISBN 978-1-4814-4687-7 (hc)

ISBN 978-1-4814-4686-0 (pbk)

ISBN 978-1-4814-4688-4 (eBook)

For Dr. Edward Kennedy,
in honor of his retirement as the beloved
principal of Seely Place Elementary School

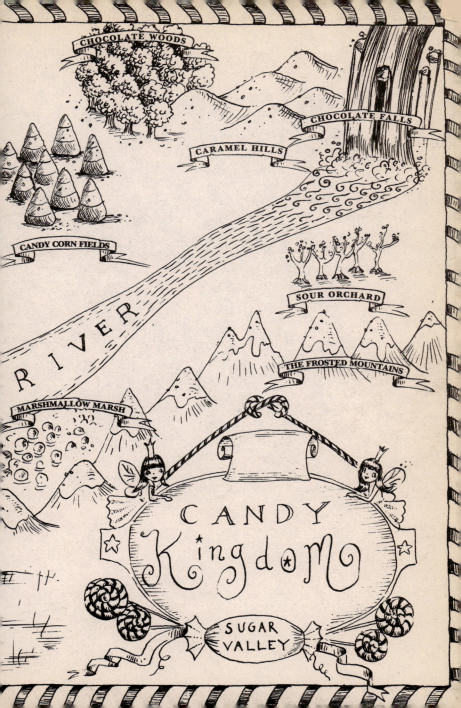

Contents

CHAPTER 1

Sun Dip Surprise

Dash the Mint Fairy fluttered her silver wings. She was enjoying sweet treats with her Candy Fairy friends on the shore of Red Licorice Lake. The sun was sliding down behind the Frosted Mountains, and she and her four friends were happy to be together. Cocoa the Chocolate Fairy, Raina the Gummy Fairy, Melli the Caramel Fairy, and Berry the Fruit Fairy were watching the colorful Sun Dip sky.

"Doesn't the sky look like a delicious painting?" Cocoa asked.

Dash swiped her finger in the air. "If I could eat a Sugar Valley Sun Dip sky, it would taste so sweet!"

"I should try to make some gummy flowers in sunset colors," Raina said.

Berry clapped her hands. "Sweet strawberries! I would want one of those gummies."

"Me too!" a voice said from above.

The five fairies looked up to see Princess Lolli and Prince Scoop. The royal couple landed next to Berry's blanket.

"Any leftover treats for me?" Prince Scoop said, smiling.

Melli jumped up and opened her basket.

"Try some of my new caramel squares," she

said. "I just made this batch today."

Prince Scoop licked his lips. "I knew this was the right place to come for some sweet Sun Dip treats!" He took a bite. "These are delicious!"

Raina made room on her blanket for Princess Lolli.

"Thank you," Princess Lolli said as she sat down. "I told Scoop that if he wanted to find you five fairies, this would be the spot." She looked over at the prince. "And if he asked nicely, he might even get a special snack."

"We're happy to share," Cocoa said. "Nothing is better than good friends at Sun Dip."

"And some candy treats!" Dash added.

 4

"I agree," Prince Scoop said. He popped one of Dash's candies in his mouth. "Dash, these treats are minty good."

Dash beamed. "Cocoa and I made them together," she said. "They are fresh chocolate mint drops. Have another!" She grinned as Prince Scoop and Princess Lolli tasted the new minty chocolate treat. She could tell from their expressions that they both liked the candy.

"Mint and chocolate are a good pair," Cocoa said, winking at Dash.

"You two work together well, and so does your candy," Prince Scoop told them.

Princess Lolli straightened out her legs and looked around at the fairies. "You five fairies always work so nicely together," she said.

"Scoop and I were wondering if you'd help us with a project."

"Sure as sugar!" all five Candy Fairies shouted.

"Wait," Prince Scoop said, holding up his hand. "You might want to know what the project is first."

Raina shook her head. "We'd be happy to help you two," she said.

"That is supersweet of you," Prince Scoop said. "We need all the help we can get."

"Some royal business?" Berry asked.

Prince Scoop nodded. "The project is in Ice Cream Isles," he told the fairies.

"Ice Cream Isles?" Dash shouted, rubbing her hand in a circle on her stomach. "Delicious!"

Prince Scoop laughed. "Yes, there are many frozen treats for you, but also some hard work." He took Princess Lolli's hand. "We are preparing to build a new castle."

Princess Lolli added, "We want to remodel the old Hall of Records. No one uses the old building anymore."

"Wow!" Raina exclaimed. "The old Hall of Records? Imagine all the books and information!"

"Most of the records and books have been moved to another place," Prince Scoop said. "We can't ask my parents to clean out the building, and Lolli and I have to go to Cake Kingdom for a few days. We need fairies we trust to help us. It's an old building and we have to be careful with the cleaning."

Dash knew Prince Scoop's parents, Queen Swirl and King Cone, would not volunteer to help clean out an old building. They were superfancy royals, and that was not their style. "Sure as sugar, we'll help!" Dash exclaimed.

"Wait, a new castle?" Berry asked. "Are you moving?"

"We will still live part of the time in Candy Castle," Princess Lolli told them. "But we need a bigger place of our own in Ice Cream Isles."

"It is going to be *sugar-tacular*!" Prince Scoop said. "Princess Lolli and I have been planning this for a while now."

"Do you have any drawings of the castle?" Cocoa asked, leaning forward.

Princess Lolli took a scroll from her bag. She carefully unrolled the plans for the new castle on the blanket. "I thought you might like to see these drawings," she said to Cocoa.

"So mint!" Dash exclaimed. She peered over Princess Lolli's shoulder. "I love the shape. It reminds me of a swirled ice-cream cone."

"Just the look we were going for," the

prince replied. "We wanted it to fit in near my parents' palace and keep the shape of the building."

"This is beautiful," Berry said. "And the inside will be superfun to decorate!"

"But remember, first we need to clean out the old hall where this cone castle will be built," Prince Scoop said.

"Scoop and I need to go to Cake Kingdom for a special cupcake dedication for Princess Sprinkle," Princess Lolli said. "If you would please get a head start on the cleaning, we will join you in a couple of days."

"Sweet!" Dash exclaimed. All the Candy Fairies loved Princess Lolli's sister, Princess Sprinkle. She was a true friend to them.

"You can count on us," Raina said.

"We'll be very careful," Melli said.

"And we will ask for lots of ice cream," Dash said, giggling.

Prince Scoop stood up. "We definitely have lots of ice cream for you," he said. "Tomorrow morning we will send Butterscotch to take you. She will meet you at Red Licorice Lake."

"Nothing is sweeter than a ride on a royal unicorn," Berry said.

"Or faster," Dash added.

Princess Lolli nodded. "Yes, you will be in the Isles by lunchtime, and Scoop's parents, Queen Swirl and King Cone, will host a royal meal for you."

"Sounds like we are getting the royal treatment," Raina said.

"Yes, you are," Princess Lolli said. "We appreciate your helping us out."

"We're glad to help," Dash said. She knew that she was speaking for all her friends.

The sun was past the top of the Frosted Mountains, and the colorful Sun Dip sky was now getting darker and darker. The Candy Fairies cleaned up their picnic and folded their blankets.

"We'll see you soon," Princess Lolli told the fairies. "Safe travels."

"Enjoy the ride," Prince Scoop called as he flew back to Candy Castle with Princess Lolli.

"We will!" Dash called back. When the royal couple was out of sight, Dash turned to her friends. "We should get a good night's rest. I have a feeling tomorrow is going to be a very big day."

"A royally big day!" Raina exclaimed.

"And we'd better all be ready," Dash said.

"Oh, we will!" Melli said. "This is going to be royally fun!"

The five friends flew off to their beds with promises to meet back at Red Licorice Lake first thing in the morning. They knew Butterscotch would be waiting. It was the start of a royal adventure.

2

A Royal Mess

Dash flew to Red Licorice Lake with a
smile on her face. The morning light made
all the candy in Sugar Valley look so delicious.
She was the first of her friends to arrive at
the meeting spot, and she saw Butterscotch.
The large royal unicorn was resting in the
shade of a tall tree.

"Good morning, Butterscotch," Dash called out. She petted the unicorn's soft caramel-colored coat. "Thank you for taking us to Ice Cream Isles this morning!"

"Thank you, Butterscotch," Cocoa said as she flew over.

Melli was by Cocoa's side. "It is a sweet day for a unicorn ride."

Raina flew above her friends and waved. "I'm ready too."

"Is that all you have with you?" Berry asked.

Cocoa and Melli turned to see Berry standing next to four large suitcases.

"Is that all yours?" Cocoa asked. She patted her little duffel bag. "This is all I brought."

"We are guests of Queen Swirl and King Cone," Berry said, with her hands on her hips. "I have to be prepared with the right clothes!"

Dash shook her head. "We're only staying a few days."

"Oh, don't get your wings all tangled," Berry said. "Butterscotch doesn't mind. And it is a good thing I overpacked. You will definitely want to borrow some of my clothes."

"I'm not sure," Dash mumbled as she climbed up onto Butterscotch's back.

"We are going to Ice Cream Isles to clean," Melli reminded Berry. "But I know what you mean about the palace being fancy. When I went up to Ice Cream Isles for the Summer Spectacular, there were formal meals with Queen Swirl at the palace. But I think this visit will be different."

"We have to eat in the palace," Berry said. "You'll see."

Raina helped Berry with her bags, and then the two of them settled into seats on Butterscotch's back.

"We're all set," Melli said to Butterscotch. "To Ice Cream Isles, please!"

Butterscotch shook her mane and stood up. The large unicorn stretched out her wings and took a flying leap up into the air.

"Nothing beats this," Dash said. "Those are some powerful wings."

"Don't get so used to this," Berry told Dash. "This is a special treat."

Dash shrugged. "I know," she said. "I am enjoying every moment of this royal ride." She looked down at the colorful candy trees and bushes in Candy Kingdom. Soon the view changed, and across the water she saw large white mountains and swirl-capped trees up ahead. Ice Cream Isles was a group of islands in the Vanilla Sea. The view took Dash's breath away.

Butterscotch took the five Candy Fairies to the Ice Cream Palace, where the fairies saw Queen Swirl and King Cone waiting.

"Hello!" the king called. He waved the Candy Fairies over to the palace entrance. "Welcome to our home," he said.

"We're so happy you could be here," Queen Swirl added. "Please come inside, and we'll have your bags sent to your room. Then we will have some lunch."

Dash could tell that her friends were

enjoying the special treatment. They followed the king and queen inside, through the large palace door. There were beautiful pieces of artwork hanging in the hallway. Dash stopped to gaze up at a painting of a queen with her hair twisted like a soft-serve cone.

"These are paintings of my parents and grandparents," Queen Swirl told Dash. "This one here is Queen Fro. She was my great-grandmother."

"I love her hair," Berry said.

Four palace guards came and flew their suitcases up the long stairway in the center of the hall. The Candy Fairies followed the king and queen into the dining room.

"We'll have a bite to eat, and then we'll show you the Hall of Records," King Cone

20

said. "It's just down the road, not too far."

"What kind of records used to be there?" Raina asked.

"Maybe some racing records or some other racing information," Dash said.

"Or some history important to Candy Fairies," Raina said, giving Dash a cold look.

"Yes, of course," Dash said, trying to cover quickly.

King Cone shook his head. "The hall has been empty for a long time. The valuable books and scrolls about the history of Ice Cream Isles have been moved to the palace. But there is still a mess in the building."

"A big dusty mess," Queen Swirl said. She rolled her eyes. "I'm not sure why Scoop wants to turn that place into a castle."

King Cone patted his wife's hand. "Scoop and Lolli want to make their own home, Swirl." He turned and winked at the Candy Fairies. "And it is a very cool space."

"Thank you for having us here for lunch," Melli said. She sat down at the long table. "This is so nice."

"We appreciate your help," King Cone said. "And we will be serving ice-cream sundaes later this afternoon," he told the Candy Fairies. "It is my favorite time of day!"

"Mine too!" Dash exclaimed. She covered her mouth. She hadn't meant her response about the ice cream to be so loud and excited. She looked over at Queen Swirl, who raised her eyebrows but didn't scold Dash for her outburst.

"Dash gets a little excited about sweet treats," Raina quickly explained.

"I see," Queen Swirl said. She took a small fan from the table and fanned her face.

King Cone winked at Dash. "I completely agree with you," he said to her. "We'll heap on some ice-cream scoops and have a big bowl of a party."

Dash was grateful for King Cone's kindness.

"We have planned an Ice Cream Fete tomorrow night so you can meet more of the fairies here in Ice Cream Isles," Queen Swirl said. "Melli, I know you have some friends here from when you visited for the Summer Spectacular."

"Yes," Melli said. "I can't wait to see Drizzle and Fluff."

Dash was looking forward to meeting the two Ice Cream Fairies whom Melli had met here. Maybe she could even race down one of the frozen mountain trails with them. *So mint!* she thought.

After lunch the Candy Fairies flew down the road with King Cone to an old stone building. Queen Swirl was right. This didn't look like a place where a princess and a prince would live.

"It is a crumbly cone, isn't it?" King Cone said.

Dash giggled. The building looked like an old cone without a scoop of ice cream.

"I know Scoop and Lolli will do wonders with this place," King Cone told them.

He took a large key from his pocket, unlocked the door, and pushed it open. Then

he reached up for a mint lantern and held up
the light to show the Candy Fairies inside.

Books and papers and maps were scattered
all over the floor. Dust was everywhere.

"No one has stepped in here for many,

many years," King Cone said. "After we moved all the records to the new location, no one has come here."

"Well, we will be able to help sort through all this," Raina said. She peered inside the room.

Dash raised her eyebrows and looked over at Melli, Cocoa, and Berry. They didn't look so excited to fly into the room.

"One paper at a time," Raina told her friends. "Let's start cleaning up."

Dash sneezed. She tried to think of the ice-cream sundaes at the palace that would be waiting for them in the afternoon. She wasn't sure that a few hours' work would get the floor cleaned up. She had never seen such a royal mess.

CHAPTER 3

Royal Treasure

The space is really big," Cocoa said as she finally flew inside the Hall of Records. "This is going to be a great home for Princess Lolli and Prince Scoop."

"I'm glad that Scoop and Lolli will be living here when they are in Ice Cream Isles. They need their own place," King Cone said.

"And I'm so pleased this old building is going to be redone."

"This place definitely needs a makeover," Berry said.

"We're just the fairies for the job, King Cone," Melli said cheerfully.

"I will leave you all to do your work," King Cone said. "See you back at the palace this afternoon for sundaes."

"Sure as sugar," Dash said.

When King Cone left, the five friends looked at one another. There was a lot of work to be done.

"Imagine what this castle will be like," Berry said, twirling around.

"It's so nice that they are creating a new castle," Melli said.

"Maybe there is going to be a new little royal!" Cocoa exclaimed.

Dash couldn't imagine Princess Lolli and Prince Scoop as parents. But then again, she could. They were both the kindest fairies that she knew. "That would be one special baby," she said.

"Do you think Princess Lolli is going to have a baby?" Melli asked.

"Maybe that is why they are redoing this space," Raina said. "And maybe that is why the five of us are getting the place ready for the renovation." She stopped and thought for a minute. "There hasn't been an announcement yet, so maybe that is why the remodeling plans are hushed."

Dash waved her hand. "You are making up

stories, Raina," she said. "No one said this was a secret mission."

"It's a possibility," Cocoa said. "Anyway, we should start straightening up." She pointed to a heap of boxes near the door. "I guess we can start picking up the papers." She reached down and picked up a book.

"Wait!" Raina shouted. "It looks like some of these scrolls are very old and might be rare. We have to be gentle."

"Okay, bossy wings," Cocoa snapped.

"You don't have to get mad," Berry said, standing between Cocoa and Raina.

Dash rolled her eyes. "We are not going to get anything accomplished if we argue," she said. "You know I like to get things done fast, so let's try to work together. We have an

 31

ice-cream sundae party to go to later, and I don't want to be late for that!"

Her friends laughed, and Dash was glad she was able to cool off Cocoa, Raina, and Berry. Melli smiled at her. Melli never liked when her friends argued.

"Raina and I will fill the boxes over there," Berry said, pointing to the other side of the room. "And you three work on this side. Then we can meet in the middle."

"Good plan," Melli said. "Let's get moving."

Dash rubbed her nose. "The dust is making me very sneezy," she said. She picked up a book and *A-C-H-O-O-O-O!* A puff of dust flew off the book she was holding. Then she sneezed again and again. And again. Her last sneeze was so powerful that she dropped the box she was holding.

"Dash!" Raina shouted from across the room.

Cocoa looked over at Raina. "Relax! Dash was only sneezing," she told her. "Can you be a little nicer?"

"Can *you* be a little careful?" Raina asked, pointing at Cocoa's slanted tower of boxes.

Cocoa huffed and turned her back. "What is it with her?" she said to Melli and Dash.

"I think Dash is allergic to the dust," Melli said, looking concerned. "You should be kinder, Raina."

"No, I think I am all right," Dash said, rubbing her eyes. She looked at the box she had sneezed out of her hands. When she bent down to gather up the papers that had fallen out, she noticed that one of the floorboards was a different color. She knelt and lifted up the board. Inside was a hiding place with a pile of old light-green leather books.

"Come look at this!" Dash cried. She picked  up one of the books to see the letters *P* and *K* in gold on the spine. She rubbed her fingers along the letters. As Dash opened the book, a puff of dust rose up. She twitched her nose and flipped through the pages.

Dash's tummy started to rumble as she saw pictures of peppermint ice cream and other frozen minty treats.

Her friends gathered around her.

"I wonder why these books were hidden," Berry said.

"There are more," Cocoa said. She reached into the hole in the floor and pulled up five more books. All of them had the same light-green leather covers. "What is *PK*? Is that some sort of Ice Cream Fairy?"

Raina scratched her head. "This is some kind of hidden treasure."

Dash picked up a book from the bottom of the pile. The cover was in better shape, and she could read the title. "I know what *PK* means!" she exclaimed. "*PK* is for 'Peppermint Kingdom'! It looks like we've found some royal peppermint treasure!"

 35

4

Mint Secrets

"Peppermint Kingdom?" Raina asked. She looked very confused. "Are you *sure*?"

Dash pointed to the cover of the book. "Yes, that is what it says on the front cover!" she said. She touched the gold lettering on the pale-green leather. "I never knew there was a Peppermint Kingdom. How mint is that?"

"As you would say," Cocoa said, "*so mint*!"

Raina took the book in her hands. "I wonder if the kingdom still exists," she said thoughtfully. She opened the book and started flipping through the pages.

"I don't know," Dash said. "But I want to find out!"

"This looks like a whole set of books," Berry said, gathering the books.

"If there are six, I think that we have them all," Dash said, counting up the books. She turned to Raina. "This was worth the trip! How minty cool to find a lost kingdom!"

Melli stood next to the pile of books. "We only found the books, not the kingdom," she said.

Dash laughed. "That's true, but if I know

Raina, she will read all these books by the end of the day. And then we'll know more."

"I'm not sure about that," Raina said, looking up at her friends. She stopped flipping through the pages. "Look at the words. This book is written in a different language. I have no idea what it says."

The friends huddled around Raina. The letters printed in the book created words that were not familiar to any of the Candy Fairies.

"What language is this?" Melli asked. "I can't make out a single word either. Except for the title, Peppermint Kingdom."

"The book must be written in some ancient Fairy language," Raina told her.

"This makes Peppermint Kingdom even more mysterious," Cocoa said.

Dash eyed the book. "What mint secrets do these books hold?" she asked.

"Let's bring one of the books back to the palace, and maybe Queen Swirl or King Cone can tell us," Berry said. "I bet no one has seen these books in a very, very long time."

"We need to clean up a little more before we leave," Melli told her friends. "We've barely made a dent in clearing the mess here."

The fairies made a line from one end of the room to the other, putting paper and trash into boxes. They worked quickly and carefully to sort out the other books and boxes scattered around the room. Soon the floor was uncovered and the books were neatly organized.

"This looks better," Berry said, slapping her

dusty hands together.

"I can't wait to hear what the king and queen have to say about the *PK* books," Dash said. "I hope they can read this language."

"Let's go ask," Raina told her.

When the five friends returned to the castle, King Cone and Queen Swirl were there to greet them.

"We found the most interesting books," Dash told the royal couple. "They were hidden under the floorboards. We're hoping that you can help us understand what the books say."

"They are written in a language we don't understand," Raina said.

Confused, the king and queen looked at the books. Then they shared a knowing look.

"In the castle's library there is an old

kingdom map," the queen said. "Come, I will show you."

The Candy Fairies followed the king and queen into the library. On the wall was a large map. Near Ice Cream Isles were the words "Peppermint Kingdom."

"So it is true?" Dash asked. Her blue eyes widened as she took in the ancient map.

"Yes, there was a Peppermint Kingdom that was part of the southern part of Ice Cream Isles," King Cone explained. He pointed to the old map. "There are a few stories about the kingdom and its sad ending."

"Sad ending?" Dash said, inching closer to the map. "What happened to all the fairies who lived there?"

"The Mint Fairies were all saved," the queen

ICE CREAM ISLES

MERINGUE ISLAND

PEPPERMINT KINGDOM

CHOCOLATE RIVER

Candy Kingdom

said quickly. "But only because the queen and king acted so fast and unselfishly."

"Oh, please tell us what happened," Dash said.

"The Peppermint king and queen and their baby had to leave their kingdom because they were in danger, and all the Mint Fairies followed them," Queen Swirl said. "Let's go into the main hall for a snack, and we can speak more."

Dash stayed back to gaze up at the map. Her wings tingled as she saw the land that was once called Peppermint Kingdom.

"Dash, come on," Cocoa called.

And with one last look back at the map, Dash flew quickly to catch up with her friends and hear more about the mysterious kingdom.

CHAPTER 5

Peppermint History

The five Candy Fairies followed Queen Swirl and King Cone into the main hall. When the hall was not being used for parties, the space was turned into a sitting room with couches and comfortable chairs in front of a large stone fireplace. Along the back wall was a long table filled with twenty different flavors of ice cream and trays filled with candy toppings.

Dash piled her bowl of ice cream high with crunchy mint treats. Then she dropped a large scoop of whipped cream on top and sprinkled some mint-chocolate flakes as a finishing touch. "Now, that is a royal sundae," she said proudly.

"Indeed," King Cone said, carrying his own bowl of ice cream. "Come, let's sit down over here, and Queen Swirl and I will tell you what we know about Peppermint Kingdom."

Queen Swirl was already seated in a large white chair. She was turning the pages in the book slowly. "I am so grateful that you found these books," she told the fairies. "It has been a long time since I've seen this language. I am trying my best to read the story, but this is a language that is no longer spoken. I studied it when I was a young fairy, but I am a little rusty."

"What is the name of the language?" Raina asked.

"The Peppermint language was very popular back at the turn of the century," the queen replied. "When I was a young fairy, we had to study the different languages of the fairies."

"But now we all speak the same language," Raina said. "When did that happen?"

"Such curious minds!" King Cone said.

Queen Swirl nodded. "Around the time of the disappearance of Peppermint Kingdom, all fairies began to speak in the same

language," she said. "This helped to unite us."

"Golly gumdrops," Raina said. "I never knew that."

"Centuries ago, the fairies were not united the way they are today," King Cone explained.

Raina stopped eating. "Are you talking about the years before the Fairy Code Book?" she asked. Raina took great pride in caring for the Fairy Code Book. The book had many stories and recipes from generations of Candy Fairies. Princess Lolli had given her the book to look after. Raina had read the book so many times. She practically had every page memorized!

"Oh, yes," Queen Swirl said. "Back in those days, there was no Fairy Code Book."

"So you are talking about a long, long, long time ago," Dash said, trying to understand.

"Yes," Queen Swirl told her. "Long before King Cone and I were even born."

"Wow!" Dash said. She licked her spoon. She smiled when she thought of the fancy king and queen as little fairies. She wondered what they had been like when they were small.

"There was an evil ogre who lived nearby," King Cone began. "He loved peppermint, and he made the Mint Fairies miserable by stealing their mint candies."

"Sounds like a sour version of Mogu," Cocoa said. She shuddered when she thought of the salty old troll who lived under the bridge in Black Licorice Swamp. The Candy Fairies had had a few run-ins with the greedy troll.

"Oh, Orni was bitterer than Mogu," Queen Swirl said.

Dash raised her eyebrows. Mogu was as greedy as trolls come! An ogre bitterer than Mogu must have been awful! "Tell us about Orni," she said.

"Orni was a small ogre with a mighty sweet tooth," Queen Swirl said. "He was clever and sticky. He caused many problems for the Peppermint royals."

Raina thought for a moment. "Who were the Peppermint royals?"

"King Leaf and Queen Mintie were the rulers of Peppermint Kingdom at the time," the queen explained. "They decided to leave their frozen mint castle here in Ice Cream Isles with their baby, Princess Min. Princess Lolli's great-great-grandparents welcomed the mint royals into Sugar Valley, and they set up Peppermint Grove so there would be mint in Sugar Valley."

"I never knew that minty fact," Dash said, licking her spoon.

"What happened to the baby?" Raina asked. "What became of Princess Min?"

"Well, she became a working Mint Fairy and went on to plant Peppermint Grove," Queen Swirl said. She flipped though the pages of the book on her lap. "What is interesting about these books is that there is more history here about the royal family."

"What happened to the Mint royals?" Berry asked.

"The king and queen made the decision to leave their throne," King Cone said. "That decision saved the lives of all the Mint Fairies, and they found a new home in Sugar Valley."

"Sweet mint," Dash said. "But there are some Mint Fairies here in Ice Cream Isles. I've had mint ice cream here."

King Cone nodded. "There have been a few Mint Fairies who came back here to the isles," he said. "Not nearly the same number as when there was a Peppermint Kingdom."

Raina put her bowl on the table and flew over to the queen. She peered at the book. "Holy peppermint!" she cried. "There's a picture here of the Peppermint queen!" She gasped.

They fairies flew over to take a look.

"I sorta look like her," Dash said, grinning.

"You more than *sorta* look like her,'" Cocoa told her.

Dash leaned in closer. "Is that a butterfly birthmark on her ankle?" she asked.

Queen Swirl nodded. "Yes, the Peppermint queen had a special birthmark. And it says here in the book that the Peppermint princess had the same butterfly-shaped birthmark on her ankle as well. It seems to be a trait of the Peppermint royal family."

Dash shrieked and dropped her bowl of ice cream on the floor.

"Dash!" Berry cried. "Watch what you are doing!"

Melli rushed to Dash and helped her clean up her mess. "Dash usually isn't so clumsy," she said to the very proper queen.

"Sorry," Dash said, fumbling to clean herself. "I was just shocked." She pulled down her sock. "You see, I have a butterfly on my ankle," she said.

There on Dash's ankle was a small butterfly-shaped birthmark.

"I never thought much about it," Dash said. She felt everyone's surprised eyes on her ankle.

Queen Swirl grinned. "I believe we have found the line of long-lost Peppermint princesses," she said.

CHAPTER 6

Royally Cool

Dash rubbed the birthmark on her ankle. She always thought the mark she was born with was cool, but *royally* cool? "This is just too weird," Dash said, looking at her ankle. The butterfly shape had always made her feel special in a way that she couldn't explain. Never had she thought this was the mark of a princess!

"Wow," Raina sighed. "It's a real sign."

"Dash is a princess!" Berry said, shaking her head. "Sweet strawberries, that is some juicy news."

Dash flew over to a window. She didn't like everyone staring at her or her ankle. She gazed out of the palace window and took in the view of Ice Cream Isles. She could see the harbor and many of the colorful cone-shaped homes. The news that there was once a Peppermint Kingdom was shocking enough. Could she really be part of the royal family? She didn't feel royal at all! "I can't be a Peppermint princess," she said. Dash turned around to face her friends and the king and queen. "How can this be? Why me?"

"Why not you?" Melli asked. "It is definitely possible. You have the same butterfly birthmark. And you are a true Mint Fairy."

"That is not a birthmark you see all the time," Cocoa told her. "It is the mark of royalty."

Dash shook her head. "I don't think this proves anything," she said. "I don't feel royal. Aren't you supposed to feel royal?"

"My dear, it is not just about *feeling* royal," Queen Swirl said. "It's about *acting* royal."

Dash turned to look out the window again. Did acting royal mean she couldn't race anymore? She felt a lump in her throat, and her wings drooped to the floor. She plopped down on the window seat.

Raina picked up another Peppermint

Kingdom book. She flew over to Dash and showed her a picture. "Dash, you look just like the princess in the book," she said. "This is more than a coincidence."

"Wow," Berry said. She sat down on the window seat next to Dash. "I can't believe I have been friends with a missing princess all this time."

"Well, I'm not really missing," Dash said. "I'm right here!" She got up from her seat. "And I am definitely *not* a princess."

Raina laughed. "What makes you so sure? You might have a long royal history. Don't you want to know the whole story?"

Dash thought about what Raina had said. Dash didn't get all excited about fashions and royal events like Berry. She didn't much care about history like Raina. She loved racing and sports. Cocoa and Melli were staring at her. What were they waiting for her to do? She was not about to start waving a royal scepter!

"If Dash is a Peppermint princess, can she bring back Peppermint Kingdom and rule?" Berry asked.

Dash was speechless. What they were saying seemed so unreal to her. Didn't they know that she didn't like wearing crowns or jewels? She didn't know how to rule a kingdom. Dash flew to the other side of the room and sank down in a large vanilla-colored chair. "I don't feel well," she said. "And I want to go home."

"This has been a lot to think about," Queen Swirl said. She flew over to Dash and put her hand on her head. "Why don't we take a rest before dinner? Princess Lolli and Prince Scoop will be here tomorrow, and we can talk about this more." She smoothed Dash's golden hair. "For now, I think you need to rest."

"Thank you," Dash said. "I would like to go rest."

"You are all staying in the sugar cone room upstairs," Queen Swirl said. "Chipper will show you the way."

Chipper was an older Ice Cream Fairy, dressed in a formal serving jacket and pants. He bowed before the queen and then before Dash.

Dash giggled. "You don't need to bow before me," she said.

"Oh, yes I do," Chipper said. He made another grand gesture and bowed again. "I grew up hearing stories of the Peppermint royals. It is my pleasure and my honor to serve you."

Queen Swirl smiled at Chipper. Dash could see that she was not going to be able to stop him. She followed the fairy up the winding staircase with her friends at her side.

"Thank you, Chipper," Dash said when he opened the door to the large room.

"Is there anything I can get you?" Chipper asked.

Dash flew inside the room. "No, thank you," she said. "We're fine. This is a *sweet-tacular* room. I'm sure we will be very comfortable here."

"She's already sounding like a princess," Berry whispered to Raina.

"I am not!" Dash shouted. She didn't think she sounded at all different. And, in fact, she didn't want to be different at all! She opened the long window in the corner and slipped out. "I need some air," she said.

"Wait," Cocoa called. "Don't go. We should talk some more."

"There are so many outfits to prepare," Berry cried.

"And royal plans to make," Cocoa added.

Dash had made up her mind. She didn't

want to talk anymore or hear stories about a missing royal family. She took off before her friends could stop her. What she needed was a fast sled on a steep slope, and she knew just where she could find one. Maybe if she got out on the slopes, she would feel more like herself. She sped away to the mountain, full speed, without looking back.

7

Minty Power

Dash flew straight to Ice Cream Mountain. In the distance she saw the trails down the mountain and her heart began to beat faster. Even from far away the sight of a mountain trail made her smile. She felt a rush from the tip of her toes to the top of her wings. Ice Cream Mountain was not as high as the

Frosted Mountains, but she could still race down the slope at top speed.

There were sleds to borrow at the mountaintop, and Dash chose a silver cone-shaped one. She thought the size and shape of the sled would be perfect for a quick ride. She added a bit of slick mint ice to the bottoms of the blades. If Dash was going to get more speed, she needed extra minty power! She strapped on her helmet and took hold of the wheel. She pushed aside all thoughts except for one—speed!

The trail was easy for Dash, and she took the turns quickly and with great control. The cool wind was pushing her hair and wings back. She loved the feeling! But her thoughts slowed her down a little. . . . Mint Fairies were spread out all over now. There were Mint Fairies in Sugar Valley, Cake Kingdom, and here in Ice Cream Isles. Was there even a need for a Peppermint princess? What would a Peppermint princess do?

Dash came to the end of the trail. She sighed. She belonged on a sled on a trail and not in a fancy ballroom for a grand occasion. She would prefer wearing a racing helmet to a crown any day!

At the bottom of the slope Dash sat in her sled and watched a couple of Ice Cream Fairies talking and laughing. They reminded her of her own friends. What would happen to their daily Sun Dips in Sugar Valley or their sweet adventures if Dash really were a princess? Would she have to live here in Ice

Cream Isles? Where? Dash shook her head. She didn't want to think about not being in Sugar Valley or with her friends. The idea was so sour. She flew off the sled and pushed it over to a long belt that would take her up the side of the mountain for another ride. Then she joined the line of fairies who were waiting to fly up the mountain for the next run.

"Want to race?" an Ice Cream Fairy asked.

"Yes! That would be *so mint*!" Dash exclaimed. The offer to race was just what she needed. Sure as sugar, a trail ride was more fun when there was a race. "My name is Dash," she said, holding out her hand.

"I'm Drizzle," the Ice Cream Fairy said. She stared at her for a minute. "Aren't you a friend of Melli the Caramel Fairy?"

Dash smiled when she recognized the Ice Cream Fairy standing in front of her. "Hi, Drizzle," Dash said. "I remember you!"

Drizzle laughed. "I definitely remember you," she said. "I got a sugar fly message this morning from Melli that she is staying at the palace. Fluff and I are planning to go over there tomorrow night for the Ice Cream Fete."

"Melli will be so happy to see you," Dash told her.

"She said that she is here on royal orders," Drizzle said.

Dash let out a sigh. There was that word "royal" again! "Well, we're here doing a favor for Princess Lolli and Prince Scoop," she said. She tried to change the subject. "Is that your sled?"

"Yes," Drizzle said. "I love racing. One day I hope to go to the Frosted Mountains. I hear those trails are tricky."

"Not so tricky," Dash said. "But minty fun. You'll have to come and race there."

Drizzle nodded. "I would love that!" she exclaimed.

The line was moving, and the two fairies flew up to their sleds at the top of the mountain. Dash couldn't wait to get on her sled. When they were racing, she wouldn't have to talk about anything royal!"

"Come, let's race," Drizzle said as they neared the top of the slope.

Both fairies got into their sleds and fastened their helmets. The second time down the trail was more fun for Dash. Now she knew the turns, and she took off superfast. Racing against Drizzle made the run much more fun!

"You are fast!" Drizzle said as she came up behind Dash at the bottom of the mountain. "I've been on this trail a ton of times and have never gone as fast as you. You are a natural."

Dash blushed. "Thank you," she said.

Hearing Drizzle tell her that made Dash's stomach flip. She was definitely born to be a racer more than a proper princess. She decided right then that she would need to explain how she felt to Princess Lolli and Prince Scoop. She didn't want to be crowned anything but the fastest fairy in Sugar Valley.

"So, what is your special candy assignment here in Ice Cream Isles?" Drizzle asked as they dragged their sleds off the trail. "I still remember Melli's hot caramel sauce for the Summer Spectacular. That was triple-scoop good!"

"My friends and I are here to help clean out the Hall of Records," Dash told her. "Princess Lolli and Prince Scoop are going to remodel the place for their new castle."

"Oh," Drizzle said, looking down. "I was hoping maybe you were here to make a mint sauce or something else minty. We don't get much mint around here."

Dash looked at Drizzle. "Really? What about mint ice cream?"

"Well, sometimes," Drizzle said. "But mint is very precious around here. There aren't many Mint Fairies in Ice Cream Isles. Sad, right?"

"Super minty sad," Dash said. She thought of the story Queen Swirl had told her.

Dash took the rope of her sled and shouted, "Race you down again!" The two fairies joined the line to fly back up the mountain, and raced again.

8

Bitter Mint Times

By the time Dash finished the last sled run, the sky was getting dark. She said good-bye to Drizzle and headed back to the Ice Cream Palace for dinner. She was surprised to find Princess Lolli and Prince Scoop sitting with her friends in the throne room.

"There you are!" Melli cried. She flew over

to Dash when she entered the room. "We were going to send out a search party for you!"

"Where have you been?" Raina said, glaring at her. "You shouldn't have flown off like that."

Dash hung her head. She knew that she had been out on the slopes a long time, but her friends should have known that she needed to race.

Princess Lolli flew over to Dash and gave her a hug. "Were you on Ice Cream Mountain?" she asked.

Dash nodded. "I'm sorry I missed your arrival. I didn't think you were coming until tomorrow."

"Don't worry about it," Prince Scoop said. "We received a sugar fly message from the palace about the Peppermint Kingdom books.

We thought it was a good idea to get here sooner." The prince paused. "We thought we'd come help you celebrate."

"Celebrate?" Dash asked. She looked around. Her friends all looked very fancy in new dresses that Dash assumed were Berry's.

"Your new dress is upstairs in your room," Cocoa told her. "Princess Lolli got us new dresses for the dinner tonight. Isn't that *choc-o-rific*?"

Dash didn't say a word. She just nodded and headed up the stairs. Even Princess Lolli and Prince Scoop were already thinking this was a Peppermint celebration.

Melli followed Dash up to the room. "Dash, are you all right?" she asked when they were alone. "We've all been worried about you."

"I met Drizzle on the slopes," Dash told her. She tried to steer the conversation a different way. "She is excited to see you tomorrow."

"I know," Melli said. "I'm excited to see her and Fluff." She handed Dash her new dress. "All this Peppermint Kingdom stuff is a lot for you, but aren't you curious to hear more of the story?"

Dash shrugged. "It may not even have anything to do with me," she said. "Unless there is a story about a speed racer." She smiled. That thought did make her happy. "Now, that would be *so mint*!"

Melli zipped Dash's dress up in the back. "You never know. Maybe there are some mint racers," she said. She stood back. "Dash, you look *sugar-tastic*!"

 78

"Thank you," Dash replied. She still didn't really feel like going downstairs to the fancy dinner.

"It might be strange to you, but I think we all want to figure out what happened to the Peppermint royals," Melli said. "It's a royal mystery."

Dash had to admit, maybe she was a little curious to hear what Princess Lolli knew about the Peppermint royal family. "Come on, let's go join the dinner party," she said.

"Thanks, Melli." She gave her friend's hand a tight squeeze.

Dash and Melli found everyone already seated in the dining hall. A large sugar-crystal chandelier hung from the center of the ceiling. It was the largest and sparkliest chandelier Dash had ever seen.

"There they are!" Berry cheered when Dash and Melli entered the room. "Now we can hear the story!"

"We were waiting for you before Princess Lolli tells us what she knows about the Peppermint royals and her family history with them," Cocoa explained.

"Oh, please tell us," Melli begged.

"Now that we're all together, I can tell you what I know," Princess Lolli said. "Long ago, my great-great-grandparents were the rulers of Sugar Kingdom. It was a bitter time for the Peppermint royals. They were battling a very strong ogre who loved mint candies."

"Anytime trolls or ogres are involved, it is upsetting," Cocoa added.

"Indeed," Princess Lolli agreed. "And this ogre, Orni, was very salty. He was stealing and making life miserable for the Mint Fairies in Peppermint Kingdom."

"My great-great-grandparents didn't know what to do," Prince Scoop said. He pointed to the painting above them. "But the Peppermint Royals knew they needed help."

Dash looked at the old painting of a king and queen and saw their kind faces. "What *did* they do?" she asked.

"Well," Princess Lolli said, "my great-great-grandparents decided that they couldn't stand by and do nothing. They called a meeting of all the royal families."

"It was very brave of them," Prince Scoop said. "The meeting was held in secret."

Raina's eyes widened. "There is no mention of this meeting in the Fairy Code Book," she said. "Or any book I have ever read!"

Princess Lolli nodded. "No one except the royal families knew about the meeting," she said. "They didn't want to let anyone, most especially the ogres, hear of their plan."

Dash looked over at her friends. Each fairy was leaning forward, waiting to hear the secret plan that the royal families came up with to save Peppermint Kingdom.

"What did they decide?" Dash blurted out. She couldn't wait any longer to hear.

Princess Lolli took Prince Scoop's hand. "The meeting lasted many hours," she said. "What they decided was very painful and difficult."

"Bitter chocolate," Cocoa whispered.

"Yes," Princess Lolli said, looking over at Cocoa. "It was very bitter for the Mint Fairies. It was decided that Queen Mintie and King Leaf would go to Sugar Valley in secret. They would no longer be king and queen. For the sake of the safety of their baby princess and all the Mint Fairies, they went to Sugar Valley as regular Candy Fairies."

"The group of Mint Fairies were not safe

here to live and to work in Peppermint Kingdom," Prince Scoop added.

"Hot caramel!" Melli exclaimed.

"There was a small group of Mint Fairies already living in Peppermint Grove at that time," Princess Lolli continued, "and so the Mint Fairies went to live with them in Sugar Valley."

"So Queen Mintie and King Leaf gave up their royal life?" Berry asked.

"Yes," Prince Scoop said. "It was very generous and brave. They did this to keep the Mint Fairies and their candies safe from the ogre."

"What happened to the ogre?" Dash asked.

"Orni moved on," Princess Lolli said. "With no mint here, he moved away, and no one heard from him again." She sighed. "These things happen with ogres."

Prince Scoop nodded. "The plan worked. He never explored Sugar Valley. Some say he sailed out on the Vanilla Sea."

"Now, that is a happy ending to a bitter mint tale," Raina said.

Dash stood up. "So it is very possible that I am related to the Peppermint royal family even though I was born in Sugar Valley," she said softly. She touched the butterfly birthmark on her ankle.

"Yes," Princess Lolli said. "Not only do you resemble the Peppermint queen, you also have the mark of the royal butterfly." She got up and flew over to Dash. "We now believe that you are the great-great-granddaughter of Queen Mintie. You could rule over Peppermint Kingdom and bring the brilliant frozen mint world back to glory."

"So mint!" Cocoa exclaimed. "Right, Dash?"

But Dash's expression was one of frozen surprise.

CHAPTER 9

Ice Cream Fete

The next morning Dash slowly opened her eyes. Her head was still swirling with all the incredible news from the day before. Dash wanted to believe that the story of the Peppermint royal family was a dream. But she knew it was real. As real as the butterfly birthmark on her ankle.

Dash saw her four friends gathered on Raina's bed in their room at the Ice Cream Palace. They didn't notice that she was awake. Dash listened to their conversation.

"I can't believe Dash is a princess!" Berry said. "After all the time we've spent together! I think that I should have known."

"How would you have known?" Cocoa asked. "Besides, Dash will be no different than she was before."

"I don't know," Raina said. "There will be many Candy Fairies and Ice Cream Fairies who will want her to be a proper princess."

"What is a proper princess?" Melli asked.

"You know, with all the royal responsibilities," Raina said.

"Will she still live in Peppermint Grove and come to Sun Dip at Red Licorice Lake?" Melli asked.

Dash opened one eye and saw Berry lean her head against the window with a heavy sigh.

"What about all those royal clothes and tiaras?" Berry added.

"I don't see Dash going for all that royal stuff," Cocoa added.

Berry snapped her head back. "Exactly! So we need to have a princess plan," she said. "We have to help Dash see that being a princess is a dream come true."

Cocoa stood up. "It might be your dream," she said, "but I don't think Dash has the same dream."

"I think Cocoa is right," Melli said. "If this isn't really what Dash wants, we should help her out."

Dash shut her eyes. She didn't want her friends to see that she was awake.

Raina flipped through the pages of a book.

"I can't believe this story is not in any book," she said. "Isn't it strange that we've never heard of Queen Mintie and King Leaf?"

"Not strange at all," Cocoa said. "It means that the plan to keep the royal family hidden worked, and that the Mint Fairies were saved."

"If Orni had tried to get to Sugar Valley, he would have probably gotten lost," Raina said, giggling. "Ogres are greedy, but not very smart. Just like trolls."

Raina's giggling got all the fairies laughing, and Dash couldn't hide that she was awake any longer. She let out a little giggle too. Then she flew over to her friends.

"Hey, Dash," Melli said. "Sorry, did we wake you?"

"No," Dash said. She didn't want to say she

had been listening to their conversation. How could she tell her excited friends that she was not as excited as they were about her new royal role?

Just then a sugar fly appeared at the window. Melli let the little messenger fly into the room, and he dropped a note in Dash's hands.

"It's an invitation to meet with Queen Swirl here in the palace tomorrow," Dash said as she read the note. "I guess we have lots to talk about," she added quietly.

"You have to accept the title of princess," Raina said. "That is how it usually works." She tapped the Fairy Code Book. "And then there will be a coronation ceremony, where you will officially become a princess."

"What if I am not sure?" Dash asked.

Cocoa stood up with a burst of energy. "Let's think about today instead," she said. "Remember, we're going to do some more cleaning at the Hall of Records, and then we're going to have the Ice Cream Fete."

"Cocoa is right," Melli said. She put her arm around Dash. "You love an ice cream feast. It's going to be fun. Drizzle and Fluff will be there too."

Dash smiled. She knew Melli was trying to cheer her up. While the Ice Cream Fete sounded delicious, she was not in the mood to celebrate.

"Let's go over to the Hall of Records now," Dash said. "After all, that is the real reason we came here."

Dash led the way to the Hall of Records.

Working on the cleaning task made her feel a little bit better. The Candy Fairies cleaned and threw out trash. When the sun started to move lower in the sky, the five Candy Fairies were done and ready for an ice cream treat.

"I can't wait to see Drizzle and Fluff," Melli said. "Tonight is going to be superfun!"

"And *sweet-tacular*!" Cocoa said, looking over at Dash. "Dash, aren't you excited about the Ice Cream Fete?"

Dash shrugged. "I guess," she said. As much as Dash wanted to join in the fun with her friends, she felt like melting into the background. All she wanted to do was go back up to their room and pull the covers over her head.

Why did they ever agree to help Lolli and Scoop and the king and queen? If they hadn't cleaned the Hall of Records, they never would have discovered the Peppermint Kingdom books, and Dash would still be just Dash the Mint Fairy and not Dash the maybe royal princess.

When the Candy Fairies returned to the palace, there were many Ice Cream Fairies arriving for the Ice Cream Fete. Drizzle and Fluff flew over to the five Candy Fairies. There was lots of hugging and excitement. But not for Dash. She was escorted to sit down with Queen Swirl. She waved to her friends sadly as they rushed upstairs to change for the fete.

Queen Swirl sat down with Dash. "Before you go upstairs and change for the party," she began, "I want to talk to you."

Dash lowered her head.

"You must let us know if we need to plan

a coronation," Queen Swirl said. "These cere-monies take planning and time. There hasn't been a crowning of a princess or prince in a very long time. This would be a grand event."

Dash gulped. She wasn't sure how to respond to the queen. Luckily, Prince Scoop flew over to her side.

"Don't pester her, Mother," he said. "There is plenty of time for all that. First, Dash needs to decide what she wants to do."

"Well, it would be best if she made a decision by tomorrow," Queen Swirl said as she turned to fly off.

Dash's wings hung down low. She felt so much pressure. Prince Scoop smiled at her and gave her shoulders a squeeze. He sat with her quietly for a while.

"Don't mind my mother," Prince Scoop finally said. "She means well. Take your time. This is a big decision."

"Do you like being a prince?" Dash asked.

Prince Scoop laughed. "Well, I didn't really have a choice," he said. "I think that you'll be a great royal." He smiled. "You are kind and understanding, and you are always ready to help your friends and others."

Dash blushed.

"If you were a Peppermint princess," Prince Scoop continued, "you could bring all the Mint Fairies together. There hasn't been a mint royal in a long time to do that. Wouldn't that be *so mint?*" He looked around. "You should get upstairs and change for the fete," he said.

"Thank you," Dash said as Prince Scoop was escorted away to mingle with all the guests.

While her friends were busy catching up with Drizzle and Fluff, Dash flew up to the guest room. She peeled off her dress and got into bed. Even though she hadn't had any ice cream, her stomach ached. She was flattered by what Prince Scoop had said, but she was scared. How could she lead the Mint Fairies? She was the smallest one! She snuggled into her bed and shut her eyes.

CHAPTER

10

A Royal Decision

The next day, just like the day before, Dash woke up before her friends. Their room in the Ice Cream Palace was silent. Dash must have been more tired than she realized, because she hadn't heard the Candy Fairies come into the room after the Ice Cream Fete. She stretched and silently got dressed. Dash didn't want to wake anyone. She knew the first thing her friends would ask would be about her royal decision. Today she would have to let the queen and king know if she was going to accept the role of Peppermint princess.

On the nightstand next to Berry's bed, Dash noticed a tiara that Berry had made. The silver piece had dozens of tiny pink sugar crystals, and it must have taken Berry hours to make. Dash flew over to the jeweled head-piece. She placed it on her head and looked at herself in the oval mirror hanging on the wall. She felt foolish. She looked silly. The tiara was too big and looked out of place on her head. Who was going to listen to her? Who was she kidding? No one was going to take her seriously as a ruling fairy princess!

Dash looked out the window at the sunrise. The sky was filled with warm orange colors.

At that moment Dash knew what she had to do. She had to fly away—and fast! She was not cut out to be a princess, and she was too embarrassed to tell anyone. She had to leave the Ice Cream Palace at once.

Dash quietly opened the window. Before she left, she looked over her shoulder at her sleeping friends. She didn't want to make them mad or worry them, so she wrote a note and stuck it on the mirror.

There was a chill in the air, but Dash didn't mind. She flew straight toward the rising sun. Below her she could see mounds of colorful ice cream and swirls of different flavors. There were not many Ice Cream Fairies up and about, and Dash enjoyed the quiet. Ice Cream Isles was a scrumptious place.

After circling the isles for a while, Dash grew tired. She landed in a white field that smelled like fresh sweet mint. The scent made her think of Peppermint Grove. She noticed a thick vine with teardrop-shaped leaves. As she got closer Dash recognized the scent. It was a peppermint plant! She settled down under the thick mint leaves and closed her eyes.

A soft breeze blew Dash's hair, and she opened her eyes. There, in front of her, was a large white unicorn with a red-and-white mane. The unicorn had a glow around her, and Dash wasn't sure if it was the sunlight or if the unicorn was actually glowing.

"Hello," Dash said. Her voice sounded thin

and weak. As she gazed at the white unicorn Dash wasn't sure if she was dreaming or if there really was a unicorn standing in front of her.

"Hello, my name is Frost," the unicorn said.

Hearing the unicorn speak startled Dash. She rubbed her eyes. She thought she must be dreaming!

"Hello," the unicorn said again.

"Hello," Dash managed to reply, very slowly. "I've never understood a unicorn before."

Frost shook her thick mane. "Only Peppermint royal family members have been able to understand my speech," she said. The unicorn took a few steps back and looked Dash up and down. "You look very familiar."

Now Dash rubbed her eyes again. Maybe she was dreaming. That would make sense.

"You seem confused," Frost went on. "I seem to have shocked you. But, to be honest, seeing you sitting here has shocked me."

Dash looked into the unicorn's eyes. "What do you mean?" she asked.

"You must be the long-lost Peppermint princess," Frost said. "I'm glad you have returned to Ice Cream Isles and to the Peppermint Castle. It has been far too long since there was a Peppermint royal living here."

Dash looked around. "There is no castle," she said.

"Ah, but there once was a castle on this very spot," the unicorn replied.

Dash leaped up. Then her eyes focused on the unicorn. "Did my friends tell you to find me and say all this to me?" she asked. She half expected the Candy Fairies to jump out from behind the cones and yell "Surprise!" She asked Frost, "What castle are you talking about?"

"Peppermint Castle," Frost explained. "It was made of pure mint. There are quite a few layers of ice cream here now, but underneath the pile of frozen treat is a castle from many, many years ago."

"That's strange," Dash said. "I've never been here before. I was just out flying and landed here." She took a deep breath. "I love the scent. It reminds me of home." She touched the leaves and then put out her hand for Frost to smell. "I love the smell of the mint leaves."

"Yes, me too," Frost replied. "You look just like your great-great-grandmother."

"You knew her?" Dash asked.

Frost spread her large silver wings. "Yes," she said. "I am very old. Unicorns live much longer than fairies."

The unicorn nudged Dash's leg and sniffed out the butterfly marking on her ankle. "Just what I thought," Frost said. "You have the royal marking. You are part of a line that cannot be broken."

The unicorn stood up and shook her red-and-white mane. Dash got a whiff of strong peppermint, like she smelled in the early spring in Peppermint Grove.

"You must be true to your destiny," Frost told her. She shook her mane once more and then took a flying leap up into the air.

"Wait!" Dash cried. "Don't go! Please come back. I have so many questions for you."

In a flash, the unicorn was gone and Dash was sitting alone under the mint leaves. She wasn't sure if what she had seen was real or not, but she had a very strong feeling that things would never be the same. She had to face the minty fact that she was a Peppermint princess.

11

A Supermint Question

Dash was about to go searching for the white mint unicorn when she heard something flying above her. She squinted up at the sky and saw her four Candy Fairy friends!

"There she is!" Cocoa cried.

"Dash!" Raina said. She came swooping down and landed next to her.

The Candy Fairy friends quickly crowded into a big group hug. Dash was shocked that they were all there. And that she was very happy to see them!

"What are you doing here?" Dash asked. "How did you find me?"

"We were so worried," Cocoa told Dash. "We had to come find you! We have been searching all over Ice Cream Isles."

"Are you all right?" Melli asked. She looked Dash up and down.

"We found your note and then went searching for you," Berry said. She put her arm around Dash. "It's a good thing Ice Cream Isles isn't as large as Candy Kingdom. I'm so glad Cocoa spotted you."

"Please don't ever go flying off like that

again. You scared us!" Melli pleaded.

Dash shot up in the air and fluttered her wings. "You are not going to believe this," she told her friends. "I understood what a unicorn said!"

"That doesn't happen every day," Melli said.

"Here?" Cocoa asked. She flew up in the air and looked around. "You saw a unicorn in this spot?"

"You met Frost the unicorn?" Raina asked excitedly. She nearly jumped on top of Dash. "Frost is the most famous unicorn ever! She might even be the oldest living unicorn."

"I guess you read that in a book," Melli said.

Raina smiled. "I did! Did you know the Ice Cream Palace has a delicious library?"

Berry moaned. "Of course you found it," she said.

"Frost says she knew my great-great-grandmother!" Dash exclaimed. She wanted to tell her friends more about her conversation with the mint unicorn.

"That's a lot of minty years," Cocoa said.

"Isn't it strange that she found me?" Dash said. She thought for a moment. "Or maybe it isn't that strange. Maybe she was meant to find me."

Melli picked up a mint leaf lying on the ground. "I think it makes perfect sense," she said. "What does she look like?"

Dash sighed and sat down on the ground. "She is *so mint!*" she exclaimed. "She has this long red-and-white peppermint mane and a silky white coat. Her wings are silver, and her eyes are as green as a mint leaf."

"Wow," Berry said. "And what did she say?"

Her friends sat down, and Dash told them about her conversation with Frost. As she spoke Dash herself couldn't believe it. "She was so . . . magical," she said. "And she smelled like fresh mint on a spring day." She sighed. That was her favorite scent of all time.

"Don't you see, Dash?" Raina asked. "You need to step up and be the princess that you are. She was telling you something important."

Melli reached out for Dash's hand. "I think this is a sign you can't ignore," Melli told her. "How many Candy Fairies get a visit from a unicorn like that? One that they can understand."

Dash hung her head. "But that's the problem," she said. "I keep telling you, I'm not a princess."

"Not all princesses love princessy things like jewels and big parties," Melli told her.

"You can bring Mint Fairies together across all the kingdoms," Raina told her. "Here and in Candy Kingdom."

Cocoa stood up. "Think of all the yummy mint frozen treats that can be made here in the Ice Cream Isles," she said. "It's a whole new minty world waiting for you!"

Dash was warming up to the idea, but still she was very unsure about what this new role would mean. Prince Scoop had said the same thing to her. She thought some more. "But what about my racing?" she asked. She looked at her friends. "And my candy in Peppermint Grove? Can I still live in Sugar Valley?"

Her friends weren't sure what to say to Dash. Dash could tell that as much as they wanted to help her, they didn't know the answers to these big questions either.

"Maybe you should talk to Princess Lolli and Prince Scoop," Cocoa finally said.

Raina grinned. "That's a great idea, Cocoa," she said. "They are royalty, so they would know."

Dash thought about Princess Lolli and Prince Scoop. They were never given the choice of whether to be royal or not. They were born into a royal family and only knew life in a castle. They were raised to rule. "How do I ask them?" Dash said. "I don't want to make them mad."

There was silence as the Candy Fairies considered Dash's comment.

Finally Raina spoke. "I think Princess Lolli and Prince Scoop would understand. You just have to be honest with them."

"Princess Lolli is so kind," Melli said. "She would definitely understand."

"Just talk to them before Queen Swirl and King Cone ask you again if there is going to be a coronation," Berry said. "Remember, today was your meeting with them."

Raina looked over at Berry and shushed her.

"Oh no," Dash said. "I missed it! Did the king and queen ask you this morning if I had made a decision?" She bit her fingernail. "You see, there is so much pressure! I know they want an answer. Only, I don't know. For the first time I don't want to be rushed! All of this is going way too fast."

"I never thought I'd hear Dash say that," Cocoa said, trying to make her minty friend smile.

"We should get back to the Ice Cream Palace," Melli said.

Dash took one more look around, hoping to spot Frost again. But she didn't see any trace of the unicorn. She flew off with her friends, back to the Ice Cream Palace—though she still wasn't sure how to answer the big super-mint question: Should she be a Peppermint princess or not?

CHAPTER

12

Peppermint Perfect

At the Ice Cream Palace there were many Ice Cream Fairies buzzing around. A row of about twenty royal palace guards with large caramel horns stood at attention. When Butterscotch flew over with the royal couple, there was a huge roar of applause.

Drizzle and Fluff waved to Dash and her

friends, and the Candy Fairies flew over.

Dash noticed how many fairies were staring at the couple as they flew down the rainbow-fruit-striped carpet.

"Princess Lolli and Prince Scoop are making an announcement," Drizzle said.

Dash's heart thumped very loudly. "What announcement?" she asked.

Drizzle unfolded the *Daily Scoop* from her bag. "Well, we don't really know, but look at the front page of the paper."

Dash took the paper and read about how all the Ice Cream Fairies were in for a royal surprise. "Sweet mint," Dash said.

"I know!" Fluff said.

Dash looked at Fluff. "What do you know?" she asked.

Fluff sighed. "Well, we all think Princess Lolli and Prince Scoop are having a baby!"

Dash breathed a sigh of relief. "Oh, we think so too," she added.

"The paper scooped the story?" Melli asked. "Now everyone knows about the baby before they had a chance to announce the news themselves."

"Part of being a royal," Berry said.

Dash didn't like the sound of that at all. Did being a royal mean no privacy and not getting to announce your own news?

"The *Daily Scoop* shouldn't have leaked the story," Raina said. "But what sugar-tastic news!" she said, giggling. "A baby!"

"I bet Princess Lolli and Prince Scoop wanted to tell their own news," Dash added.

"But news of their baby is everyone's news," Raina said. She pointed to the fairies. "Look at all the fairies who have come to show how happy they are!"

Dash was overwhelmed by the number of Ice Cream Fairies lining the palace gardens. There was lots of cheering. Raina was right. There certainly were many happy fairies around.

Prince Scoop and Princess Lolli flew up to a landing above the front door of the palace, decorated with large swirled ice-cream cones and rainbow lollipops.

"Thank you all for being here," Prince Scoop told the crowd. "We wanted to clear up some rumors about us."

The cheering stopped, and everyone grew quiet.

"Princess Lolli and I are going to have a baby!" he declared.

The crowd cheered loudly.

Princess Lolli blushed. "Thank you for being so excited about our little one," she said. "We hope you will welcome our baby and help us keep Ice Cream Isles and Candy Kingdom in sweet shape for the future!"

There was a loud thundering of applause.

"Aren't they so sweet?" Fluff said, sighing.

Dash thought how lucky all these Ice Cream Fairies were that they got to have Princess Lolli around. "No one is sweeter than Princess Lolli," she said.

"We're so happy that Prince Scoop married her," Drizzle added.

Melli gave her Ice Cream Fairy friends a big hug. "We'll see you later," she said. "Right now we need to fly to meet the royal family."

Dash was glad that Melli didn't tell Fluff and Drizzle all about the Peppermint princess business. Dash wasn't quite sure what she would tell them!

The five Candy Fairies were shown into the throne room, where Princess Lolli and Prince Scoop greeted them.

"We're so happy for you," Raina said, speaking for them all. "You are going to be the best parents."

"Thank you," Princess Lolli said. "I'm sorry we didn't tell you first. We looked for you this morning, but you must have been exploring."

The Candy Fairies shared a secret glance.

"I bet there's an ice cream feast waiting for us inside the castle," Prince Scoop said with a grin on his face.

For the first time ever, Dash didn't really want ice cream.

Melli saw Dash hesitate. "We'll get you some ice cream," she said. "Maybe you want to speak to Princess Lolli and Prince Scoop."

Dash was grateful for the alone time with the princess and prince. She flew with them over to a quiet corner of the room.

"I heard from my parents that you haven't made a decision," Prince Scoop said to Dash.

Dash felt her face get warm and cherry red. "I was supposed to meet with your mother," she said. "I am not sure what to tell her yet."

Princess Lolli took Dash's hand. "What do you make of all this Peppermint princess business?" she asked.

"I don't know," Dash said slowly. "Honestly,

I feel a little funny about all of it."

"That is understandable," Prince Scoop said. "It is not every day that you hear you might be the princess of a frozen land."

"A *minty* frozen land," Princess Lolli added.

They sat down in the throne room to talk more. Dash sat between the royal couple and felt her wings relax.

"Everyone is very excited about this news," she told them. "And I'm not sure how I feel."

Princess Lolli nodded. "You've been given a great surprise." She smiled at Dash. "But a truly *sweet-tacular* surprise."

"You can help build up the mint ice cream and mint toppings here in Ice Cream Isles," Prince Scoop said. "We always look for more minty flavors and toppings."

Dash liked the thought of creating new flavors and minty frozen treats. There were so many new things to try. Maybe being a mint princess *was* more than planning a party.

"You know, Lolli doesn't enjoy planning parties nearly as much as Sprinkle does," Prince Scoop said, smiling.

Princess Lolli laughed. "That is true!" she exclaimed. "Being a fairy princess is not always perfect, but you can make a difference and really help others." She smiled. "But, Dash, if you decide to have a coronation, Sprinkle wouldn't miss it!"

"Everyone is excited," Prince Scoop told Dash. "There has not been a coronation in Ice Cream Isles since my father received his crown as a young fairy."

"Wow," Dash said. She was beginning to understand why this coronation was such a big deal. Dash took a moment to think. She thought about minty cool things she could do as princess. She could have a royal national race. She could make a special holiday for mint. She could really help some of the Mint Fairies and Ice Cream Fairies create candies and frozen treats. These things were starting to make sense to her . . . and make her excited.

Then Dash thought of Frost, her family history, and her responsibilities.

"I will be crowned the princess of Peppermint Kingdom," Dash said, proud and strong.

"Dash, you will make a perfect Peppermint princess," Princess Lolli told her, giving her a hug. "Perfect in your own way."

The Candy Fairies returned with bowls of ice cream.

When Cocoa saw Dash smiling and hugging the princess and prince, she perked up. "You decided to be crowned the Peppermint princess!" she cried.

"Yes," Dash said, giggling.

"There is so much to be done!" Berry cried. "New dresses and all the details for the coronation!"

Dash rolled her eyes. "Berry, relax. That isn't the most important part of the corona-tion." She looked over at Princess Lolli and Prince Scoop, who gave her a nod and a warm smile. "The crown doesn't make the princess," she said.

"But the princess has to get the crown," Berry added. "And that is a huge party!"

Dash had a feeling that Raina, Berry, Cocoa, and Melli would be on the planning committee and make sure the party would be grand. Dash just had to hold on for the ride!

CHAPTER 13

Hidden Mint Home

Dash was right about her friends being excited for the Peppermint princess coronation party. For the next few days her friends, and everyone else in the kingdom, were busy making plans and discussing dresses and decorations. The only thing that interested Dash was the menu for the party *after*

the crowning. Never had she heard of such a minty lineup of candies and ice cream flavors! A Peppermint princess crowning meant lots of sweet mint treats.

Dash kept busy by meeting with Mint Fairies who lived in Ice Cream Isles, and with Queen Swirl and Princess Lolli. Dash was interested in ideas about new mint candies and ice cream flavors.

"Dash, you are a natural at this," Queen Swirl said. "You listen and advise like you have always been a princess."

Dash looked at Princess Lolli. "I have watched and learned from the best," she said. "I hope that I can rule like Princess Lolli."

"Thank you, sweet Dash," Princess Lolli said, giving Dash a squeeze. "You are not alone. Peppermint Kingdom is part of Ice Cream Isles. So we will be here for you."

At Dash's princess dress fittings, Berry and another fairy took her measurements. At each fitting Dash was just shown parts of the dress. She wasn't sure how the final gown would look. Berry wanted it to be a surprise.

Finally, the night before the coronation, Berry flew in with a large package. All the Candy Fairy friends gathered around in their room in the Ice Cream Palace. Berry opened the box and held up the dress.

At the first sight of her very first princess gown, Dash gasped. "That's mine?" she asked. "It's *so mint*!"

Berry was beaming. She held up the dress

for Dash to see it better. "I hope you like it."

Dash flew over to Berry and flung her arms around her neck. "I love it!" she cried. The dress was made of beautiful cotton-candy-pink, green, and white. It looked like a fresh beautiful mint candy.

"Try it on!" Cocoa said.

Dash slipped the dress on. It fit perfectly! She twirled around, and the fluffy skirt fell gently around her legs.

"You look scrumptious," Melli said. "A true mint princess."

"Thank you, Berry." Dash hugged her friend again. "This is the sweetest dress ever. I am very proud to wear it."

Berry blushed. "You deserve it," she said. "And I also made these sugar-crystal hairpins for your hair." She held open her hand for Dash to see.

"*Sugar-tastic!*" Dash exclaimed.

"Tomorrow is going to be a great day," Raina said to Dash.

"I think every fairy will be there to celebrate," Melli said. "All the fairy kingdoms will be there."

There was silence in the room as Dash felt her face grow pale.

"We'll all be with you," Cocoa said quickly. "It's going to be *choc-o-rific*, you'll see."

Dash took off her dress and hung it carefully on the hanger. She had a funny feeling in her stomach.

"We should let you get some rest," Cocoa said. "We have one more thing we need to do for tomorrow." She nodded to the other three fairies.

"Will you be all right here?" Melli asked.

Dash flew into bed. "Yes," she said. "Thank you for everything."

When her friends had left, Dash began to wonder how things would be different once the ceremony happened. Would she see her friends as much? Would she know the right things to say? And how to act?

Dash stood in front of the window and looked out to the horizon. The sky was glittering with stars. But then she couldn't believe what she saw and rubbed her eyes. Frost was flying toward her!

Frost landed on the balcony outside Dash's room. "Come with me," the unicorn instructed.

Dash flew out to her. "I really don't have that much time," she said. "But I am so happy to see you!" She gave the white unicorn a big hug. "I have so many questions for you."

Frost spread her wings, and Dash jumped onto her back. She held on to Frost's long red-and-white mane. Higher and higher they flew, until the Ice Cream Palace looked like a small toy.

"Where are we going?" Dash asked.

"You'll see," Frost replied. The unicorn flew up to the top of Ice Cream Mountain, where Dash had been sledding. Only this time, they flew to the other side of the mountain, where there were no trails.

The smell of fresh mint was so strong and delicious! The large white moon gave plenty of light for Dash to see.

"Is that mint frosting?" Dash asked. She looked at the beautiful heaps of white mint frosting layered on the mountainside.

"Yes," Frost replied. "And this was Queen Mintie's favorite place in Peppermint Kingdom."

"Really?" Dash asked. "I can see why." She flew off Frost's back and looked around. "And it's so close to the slopes!" she exclaimed.

Frost threw her head back and laughed. "Just like Queen Mintie," she said.

Maybe racing and royalty had both been passed down to Dash from Queen Mintie.

"There will be so many people at the coronation tomorrow," Dash said. "I really don't like crowds and people looking at me. Except when I'm racing. Then I don't mind at all, because I am going so fast."

Frost nodded. "You will make so many fairies happy and proud," she told Dash. "This is bigger than just you."

Dash hadn't thought about the coronation in that way. She thought of all the Mint Fairies back in Sugar Valley and Ice Cream Isles.

"This coronation is about more than just

you getting a crown," Frost told her. "It is about all the Mint Fairies having a princess."

Frost's words were so helpful to Dash. Suddenly she didn't mind all the crowds. "I need to get back so I can sleep," she said. "I have a coronation tomorrow!"

14

A Secret Mint Book

The next morning, when Dash woke up, she saw her friends gathered around the table by the window. They must have gotten up very early, because they were already wearing their fancy dresses for the coronation. At first Dash was concerned that something might be wrong. They were all huddled together as if they were set on fixing a problem. But then she saw Cocoa smile.

"Dash, you're awake!" Cocoa said. She flew over to her. "We've been waiting for you to get up! You were asleep when we came in last night, and we wanted to let you sleep late."

"We have a special gift for you," Raina told her. "Come over here so we can show you."

"You already did so much for me," Dash said.

Raina flew over to her and took her hand. "This is a special surprise!" she exclaimed.

Still half asleep, Dash flew between Cocoa and Raina. Dash saw an old red-and-white leather book on the table. She bent over to get a closer look.

"We found this in a pile of books from the

Hall of Records," Berry said. She handed the book to Dash.

"We wanted to keep it a secret until today," Cocoa said. "We thought this was the perfect coronation gift."

The book was very old, and Dash handled it with great care. She could tell her friends were bursting with excitement. When she opened the cover, Dash smelled a faint scent of mint. "How old is this?" she asked.

"Read the first page," Melli told her.

"Luckily, this book is written in a language we can read," Raina said, grinning. "I think Queen Mintie wanted to make sure her descendants could read it."

Inside, on the first page, was beautiful script writing. "Queen Mintie's diary!" Dash said. She turned a few more pages. "Oh, this *is* the best gift ever!"

"A good book is always a good idea," Raina said. "Especially one that tells your family history."

"Queen Mintie wrote in this book when she planned to leave Ice Cream Isles and head to Sugar Valley to hide," Cocoa told her.

"*So mint,*" Dash said, sitting down to read the first entry. "It's as if the queen is talking to me." She looked up at her friends. "Thank you for finding this."

"Now you can hear the story in the queen's own words," Berry said.

Raina put her hand on Dash's shoulder. "Queen Mintie and King Leaf weren't running away because they were scared. They were planning for the future of the Mint Fairies."

"They were hoping for someone like you to find this diary," Cocoa said. "And we're so proud of you. You are our Peppermint princess."

Dash burst into tears. Not because she was sad, but because she was so happy.

"Tell her the best part!" Melli said.

"There's more?" Dash asked, wiping her eyes.

"Yes," Cocoa told her. "We found out that

Queen Mintie was a small but speedy racer too. She had the Peppermint Castle built into the peppermint-frosted side of the mountain so she could race her sleds."

Berry flipped to a page near the end of the book. "And look, there is a picture of the castle."

"Buried under layers of frozen peppermint," Cocoa added. "Just imagine all the hot cocoa it will take to melt that mint!"

"And how *sugar-tacular* the frozen castle will be once it is fixed up," Melli added.

"I heard something about all that," Dash said, looking out the window.

"Look at these drawings," Cocoa said, pointing to the pictures in the queen's diary.

Dash looked closely at the drawings.

 149

Peppermint Castle looked so beautiful.

"There will be two more castles in Ice Cream Isles," Melli said with a grin. "One for Princess Lolli and Prince Scoop, and one for the Peppermint princess."

Cocoa went to the window and pointed to the mountain. "You can be like Princess Lolli and Prince Scoop and have two homes," she said. "One in Sugar Valley and one here."

"I know," Dash said. She was getting more comfortable with the idea of living in both kingdoms. "I plan to have you all come and stay with me. Being in a castle alone is not nearly as fun as being there with your friends."

"Sure as sugar!" Berry shouted.

"We aren't going to say no to that invitation!" Cocoa said.

"I know you will have the sweetest treats," Melli said, giggling.

"And a whole room of sleds!" Raina exclaimed.

The bells in the large bell tower outside in the royal garden began to ring. It was the call to start the procession for the coronation at the palace.

"We'd better get you ready," Berry said.

Dash slipped her new dress on and sat on the cotton candy pouf while Berry and Raina styled her hair. She was already feeling like a princess.

"Oh, Dash," Berry said. "You look good enough to eat!"

Dash giggled. "Thank you," she said. She peered into the mirror. "I love the peppermint clips. You both are the best."

"That is a *sweet-tacular* compliment, coming from a princess," Berry said, smiling.

"Now I have to wait for my ride." Dash looked out the window, and sure enough, there was Frost. She landed on the balcony and waited for her princess.

The five Candy Fairies stood in awe of the beautiful unicorn. Dash stepped forward and introduced her friends to Frost. She turned to them. "Please ride with me," she said.

"Are you sure?" Berry asked.

"Sure as sugar," Dash said. "I want you to be next to me during the whole ceremony. You are my royal set of friends." She smiled.

"You have beautiful new dresses too."

Raina, Berry, Cocoa, and Melli flew up and settled on Frost's back.

It was time for the Peppermint princess to make her entrance, with her royal friends at her side.

15

The Hidden Crown

From her palace window, Dash looked down at the crowds flying in for the coronation. She knew there would be many fairies coming to the event, but never did she imagine the tremendous crowd around the front gates.

"Holy peppermint," Dash said softly. Her heart was pounding so fast!

"Wow! The gardens look *so mint*!" Cocoa exclaimed.

Peppermint frosting and peppermint candies were spread across the front of the palace. Tiny green-and-white and red-and-white candies were hanging down on thin licorice threads. The palace looked like a frozen peppermint painting.

"Wait until you see the inside of the ballroom," Raina said. "That is what we were doing last night. It was so much fun, and the room looks minty fresh."

Dash took a deep breath. As she flew down to the ballroom she got a strong whiff of all the fresh mint. The calming scent of peppermint helped steady her nerves. That and gripping Cocoa's hand!

"Hello!" King Cone said. He and Queen Swirl were standing at the entrance to the throne room, next to the ballroom. "Today is the day! And you look beautiful."

"You look peppermint perfect," Queen Swirl added. "Please come inside the throne room. We want to show you something."

Dash couldn't take her eyes off the crowns on the king and queen. For the coronation they were wearing their fanciest crowns and outfits. Princess Lolli and Prince Scoop were there, also dressed in fancy royal crowns and clothes. Once they were inside the throne room, King Cone held up a long scepter.

"This has been in our royal family for centuries," the king proudly told her. He pointed to the ball on the top. "If you look closely, you will see sweet treats from each part of Sugar Valley and colors of every flavor of ice cream."

Dash stared at the bright candies and colors. She had never seen anything so bright and beautiful.

"With this scepter I will be able to bestow the title of princess on you," the king explained. "I will touch one shoulder and then the other." The king gently touched Dash's shoulders with the royal scepter. He nodded to the queen at his side.

Queen Swirl was holding a box, and she gave it to Princess Lolli. The box was green and white with tiny mint swirl drawings. It looked very old and dusty. "What's inside?" Dash wondered.

"This is the Peppermint crown that has been hidden for many years," Princess Lolli told her. "This crown was put away here when it was too dangerous to rule. But it is time this crown is placed on a Peppermint princess and the reign of the Peppermint Kingdom continues."

Dash's eyes widened as Lolli lifted the crown out of the box. She couldn't believe the crown was for her. She had a hard time believing *all* of this was for her!

"It's time to go into the ballroom," Prince Scoop said.

"We will see you in there," King Cone told the Candy Fairies. He took Queen Swirl's hand, and they flew out of the room.

Cocoa was still holding Dash's hand. She

gave a squeeze, and Dash felt more relaxed. It was so nice to have her four friends with her. Together, they flew down the long green fruit-leather carpet to the stage at the end of the ballroom.

"Keep your eyes on the king and queen," Raina whispered to her.

Dash did as Raina told her. She tried not to look around at all the fairies in the ballroom. But she did see that Princess Sprinkle was seated in the front row! Dash flew up the center aisle and straight to the spot in front of the king and queen.

"Welcome, everyone," King Cone said in a booming voice. "It is my great privilege and pleasure to welcome you. Today is a day we will remember for years to come. It is the day

that we celebrate our history and our new Peppermint princess."

The crowd roared with excitement. Dash giggled. She was so nervous! Just as the king had told her he would, he showed the crowd the scepter. Dash lowered her head.

"It is by the power vested in me as the King of Ice Cream Isles," the king said, "that I declare you, Dash, the Peppermint princess of Peppermint Kingdom."

A flurry of white mint flakes fell from the ceiling in celebration.

Dash hugged her friends, Princess Lolli, Prince Scoop, and even the king and queen. "Thank you," she said. She touched her peppermint crown. She had never felt so proud.

A green curtain rose on the other side of the room. On the stage were the Yum Pops! They were the Candy Fairies' favorite band. The catchy melody of their new song, "Peppermint Perfect," filled the room.

"This is the grandest, mintiest party ever!" Dash exclaimed.

Queen Swirl and King Cone beamed at Dash. "We couldn't be prouder of you," King Cone told her. "You are true mint, and we're thrilled to have you as our sweet Peppermint princess."

"Long may you reign!" Queen Swirl exclaimed.

Dash grinned. She looked out of the large windows in the ballroom. Outside, she saw Frost. She loved knowing that Frost had known her relatives and that she was there to share the day with her.

Frost threw her head back, and her long red-and-white mane looked beautiful. Now Dash had her own royal unicorn!

"Let's eat some mint!" Dash declared.

Her friends cheered and flew off to the buffet tables filled with special mint treats.

The day continued with lots of dancing and eating a whole lot of mint. The coronation was a perfect peppermint party.

Dash's new adventure as a princess had begun!